DISCOVERIES
IN THE OVERWORLD

DISCOVERIES IN THE OVERWORLD

LOST MINECRAFT JOURNALS BOOK ONE

Winter Morgan

Sky Pony Press
New York

Copyright © 2015 by Hollan Publishing, Inc.

All rights reserved. No part of this book may be reproduced in any manner
without the express written consent of the publisher, except in the case
of brief excerpts in critical reviews or articles. All inquiries should be
addressed to Sky Pony Press, 307 West 36th Street, 11th Floor, New York,
NY 10018.

Sky Pony Press books may be purchased in bulk at special discounts for
sales promotion, corporate gifts, fund-raising, or educational purposes.
Special editions can also be created to specifications. For details, contact
the Special Sales Department, Sky Pony Press, 307 West 36th Street, 11th
Floor, New York, NY 10018 or info@skyhorsepublishing.com.

Sky Pony® is a registered trademark of Skyhorse Publishing, Inc.®,
a Delaware corporation.

Minecraft® is a registered trademark of Notch Development AB.
The Minecraft game is copyright © Mojang AB.

Visit our website at www.skyponypress.com.

10 9 8 7 6 5 4 3 2 1

Library of Congress Cataloging-in-Publication Data is available on file.

Cover photo by Megan Miller

Print ISBN: 978-1-5107-0350-6
Ebook ISBN: 978-1-5107-0353-7

Printed in Canada

TABLE OF CONTENTS

DISCOVERIES
IN THE OVERWORLD

1
DISCOVERIES

I think I see diamonds!" Harriet called out from where she was digging.

"Where?" asked Jack, pulling his pickaxe out of the block he'd been breaking.

Toby had been mining with an iron shovel nearby, but he stopped and walked over to Harriet. "Where are the diamonds? I don't see any blue."

The group had just started their planned treasure-hunting excursion through the Overworld, when they had spotted an abandoned mineshaft and stopped to mine for diamonds. Diamonds are extremely valuable trading resources in the Overworld, and finding some would be a great start to their treasure hunting.

"Look, it's blue!" Harriet pointed to a cluster of diamonds in the mine. She picked up as many as she could and handed some to her friends. "We have to store these in our inventories."

"I can't believe we really found diamonds," said Toby. It was becoming increasingly difficult to find diamonds in the Overworld, and this was a lucky find.

When they placed the last gemstone in their inventories, Harriet dug her pickaxe deep into another layer of the mineshaft. But Toby just stood there. "I doubt we'll find any more diamonds here. We should just take what we have and move on."

"Seriously?" Harriet kept digging deeper.

"Yes," insisted Toby. "We should stick to our plan. We want to reach the jungle before nightfall."

Jack held a map in his hands. "It looks the jungle is still far away. We should leave. I hear there's a lot of treasure there."

Harriet was annoyed. "We don't even know if there's a jungle temple with treasure. But we do know that there are diamonds in this mineshaft."

"I think we've already unearthed all the diamonds." Toby looked over his inventory.

Harriet and Toby would have kept arguing, if Jack hadn't interrupted. "Watch out!"

Silverfish crawled on the floor toward them. They put their pickaxes away and grabbed their diamond swords to strike at the swarm.

"There are so many of them," Harriet called out as she swung her sword at the seemingly endless silverfish crawling at their feet.

"Should we search for a spawner?" asked Jack.

"I'm not sure," Harriet replied breathlessly. "I think we need to destroy these first."

The group used all of their strength to battle the silverfish, until the room went still. "I think I got the last of them," said Jack.

Looking around for any last stragglers, Toby spotted something in the corner of the mineshaft. "Hey, what's that?"

The trio walked over to the corner, and Harriet said, "It looks like an enchanted book. That will come in very handy for our treasure hunting!" She leaned over to pick it up and leafed through the first few pages of the book. "This isn't an enchanted book at all. It looks like somebody's journal."

"Do you think somebody is living in this mineshaft?" Jack looked around the dark and creepy mineshaft for a bed.

Harriet studied the book. "No, I think this journal is old."

"Who wrote it?" asked Toby as he stood behind Harriet trying to get a good look at it.

Harriet turned the book to look at the journal's spine. "I don't know. But it has a warning on the cover! It says, 'Do not open this book! Anyone who reads this will be cursed'!"

"Really? Let me see," said Jack.

Toby laughed. "What a threat. How would they know if we read it?"

Jack didn't see anything funny about it and didn't understand why Toby was laughing. "I wouldn't laugh—curses should be taken seriously. Reading this book could be really dangerous."

"You're such a scaredy-cat! Nothing is going to happen to us if we just read it," said Toby.

"How do you know?" Jack countered.

"Because there are no such things as curses. Right, Harriet?"

Harriet hesitated. She wanted to agree with Toby, but she wasn't totally one hundred percent sure. She had never read a book that had a warning on its cover. She was conflicted. "I'm not sure. Although, I've never been cursed, I can't know that curses don't exist."

Toby grabbed the book from Harriet's hands. "Well, unlike both of you, I'm not afraid to read it."

"Toby, don't!" shouted Harriet. She was more afraid than she'd realized.

Jack looked nervous.

Toby was about to open the journal anyway when a silverfish crawled next to his foot and bit him. "Ouch!"

"Watch out!" Harriet lunged at the silverfish with her diamond sword. "Jack was right—the book is cursed! Put it back!"

Toby glared at her. "That silverfish has nothing to do with me reading the journal. It's just a coincidence."

Harriet wanted to believe Toby. He made sense, but she was still worried. The book didn't say what exactly would happen if they read it, so she began to imagine all sorts of ways they could be cursed. "What if we read the journal and are destroyed by a creeper and respawn in the Nether?"

"That's impossible. We weren't even in the Nether." Toby held the book open in front of him.

"Please don't read it," begged Jack.

"I am going to read it now, just to prove that you can't be cursed from reading a book."

"But that's somebody's personal journal," said Jack. "Even if we aren't cursed, it's still wrong to read someone's private writing."

Toby paused for a moment. He knew Jack was right. He wouldn't want anyone reading his diary. In fact, he'd never let anyone know he even kept a diary. That was a secret. It was full of all the things he could never to say to other people in real life. He closed the book.

"Thank you." Harriet let out a sigh of relief.

"Why do you think this person"—Toby looked at the cover—"William the Explorer, left his personal journal in this abandoned mineshaft?"

Jack stared at him. "Did you say William the Explorer?"

"Yes." Toby pointed to the very bottom of the cover. "The Journal of William the Explorer."

"Haven't you heard of him before?" asked Jack.

Harriet and Toby stood silently, watching Jack. Toby looked down at the brown journal.

"William the Explorer was the greatest explorer in the Overworld, ever. He went missing a long time ago. People have been searching for him for ages. Nobody has been able to find him. That journal will be very valuable. Maybe it can even lead us to him!"

"Does this mean you want me to read it?" Toby was confused.

Jack paused. He was too excited about having discovered the journal of the famous William the Explorer to worry about curses. "I think we have to read it. Maybe it can help us find him. He may have left it here as clue to his whereabouts."

"What if he doesn't want to be found?" asked Harriet.

"Everybody wants to be found," said Jack.

"Okay, let's read it!" Harriet was quick to give in. She was curious too.

Toby began to read the first page of the journal aloud to his friends. They hovered over him, staring at its worn-out pages as they listened.

2

JOURNAL ENTRY: WARNINGS

If by chance someone stumbles upon this journal, they should burn it. Others should never read what I write in here. This book chronicles my explorations in the Overworld, and only exists so I can study my past trips. Like any good explorer, I keep a journal of all my finds. This book is for my eyes only. If you find yourself in possession of this book, please return it to me or burn it. If you do read it, you'll be cursed. You must take this warning quite seriously. Please stop reading right now. Please put the book down, and do not continue to the next page. You will suffer at great costs if you continue to read the following pages.

I know what I wrote is a bit repetitive, but as my friend Oliver always says, "Sometimes you have to repeat yourself to be heard." Please listen to my words and close the book. You were never meant to read it.

Trip 1: Exploration to the Cold Biome

Today Oliver and I reached the top of a mountain in the cold biome. It felt as if we were never going to reach the mountain's peak, but when we did, we were rewarded with stunning views of our old hometown. As we looked down at the town, we both admitted that we missed home.

Oliver asked me, "Do you think we made the right decision?"

I didn't know how to respond. I had been pondering the same question for a long time. It was a hard decision to leave home to explore the Overworld, but that was our dream. We wanted to map the world so that others could follow in our footsteps. We wanted to open up the Overworld so that everyone could enjoy it.

Oliver's a map expert and also an alchemist. He knows how to brew all kinds of potions, and he's also very good at spotting ingredients for them. I'm more of a fighter. A warrior. A griefer once summoned an army of zombies and skeletons to attack the villagers in our town. I helped protect our people and led the town to a victory. I am not afraid to fight for what is fair. But I never attack unless I'm provoked. We were a good team together.

As we trekked through the snowy landscape, another pair of explorers approached us. I recognized one of them. His name was Charles, and he had spent some time in our village after one of his long expeditions. I remembered asking him about the trip and all the places he had seen. His travels had inspired me to become an explorer.

"Charles," I called out, but whe he turned around, he didn't seem to recognize me.

"Hello?" Charles's sword was out; he didn't know if I was a friend or a foe. In either case, he was ready to attack.

"It's William," I explained. "You spent some time in my town—we talked."

Charles paused. "Yes, I remember you. What are you doing in the cold biome? This is fairly far from your home."

"I'm also an explorer."

Charles seemed surprised. "You're an explorer? But my friend Thao and I are the only explorers of the Overworld."

"Well, not anymore," I replied, but as these words fell from my mouth, I realized they might have sounded a bit cocky. So I guess I can say I wasn't surprised when Charles and Thao came at Oliver and me with their diamond swords.

"Ouch!" I shouted and rushed to strike Charles with my sword. "Why are you attacking me?"

"I discovered the cold biome and I am placing it on a map!" Charles roared as he slammed his diamond sword against my arm. I was losing hearts dangerously fast.

"Okay. Take credit for this cold biome." I could barely spit out these words.

Charles put down his sword. "I will destroy you if you continue to explore the Overworld. We are the only explorers and we don't need any competition."

I looked over at Oliver, and he nodded his head.

Oliver said, "Okay—you can be the only explorers in the Overworld."

Charles looked at me. "Are we in agreement, William?"

I also nodded my head. "Yes, we'll go home."

They put down their swords, and Oliver and I walked away, headed toward our town.

As soon as we were safely out of sight, I said to Oliver, "Let's make a left and explore. I hear there's a large desert in this part of the Overworld."

"But we promised Charles that we wouldn't," said Oliver.

"We can't go back to our town. It's our dream to explore. We can't let Charles bully us and stop us from exploring. He doesn't own the Overworld."

Oliver thought about it and then nodded his head slowly. "Okay," he said. "Let's do this." We turned left and began our trek toward the desert. We didn't know our lives were about to change forever.

3
FINDING WILLIAM
THE EXPLORER

What happened next?" Harriet asked Toby.

Toby put the journal down. "That was the end of the first entry. Would you like me to read more? It looks like the next entry is about Oliver." He scanned the pages. "I think Oliver goes—"

Jack cut him off. "Don't tell us anything unless you're going to read the entire entry. We want to know everything. Don't just read excerpts."

"Okay, I'll keep reading." Toby opened the book, but before he could read the first word aloud, they were interrupted by an army of skeletons entering the abandoned mineshaft.

"We have to get out of here!" Harriet shouted as she shot an arrow toward the bony beasts pouring into the mineshaft.

"It must be night!" Toby called out. "And we never built a shelter. This is awful."

Jack splashed potions on the skeletons, which weak-ened the hostile mobs. Harriet ran toward them and attacked with her diamond sword. The wobbly skeletons began to fall. "I think we're going to win this battle!" she shouted.

"Not so fast!" Toby shouted. A new horde of zombies lumbered toward the group.

Jack kept throwing potions, but the zombies were persistent. One zombie walked over to the journal.

"Stop him!" Harriet shouted to Toby as she fought off the monsters that surrounded her.

Toby lunged at the zombie and destroyed him with one blow from his enchanted diamond sword. He picked up the journal and placed it in his inventory.

"The journal is safe," Toby shouted to the group.

"But we're not!" Jack cried as he battled the exhaust-ing mobs. Two creepers floated in and exploded by the skeletons. Things were getting out of control.

Toby raced to Jack's side and helped him battle the zombie and skeleton invasion. Jack had just destroyed one last particularly vicious skeleton when he realized he couldn't see Harriet in the mineshaft. "Harriet?" he called out nervously. He was worried his friend had been destroyed.

"I'm here," her voice called back.

Jack couldn't see Harriet anywhere. "Where? Where are you?"

Her voice grew louder. "I'm right behind you."

Jack turned around, but there was still nothing but empty mineshaft. "Where?"

Harriet tapped him on the shoulder. "Guys, you should drink a potion of invisibility. Then we can sprint out the exit and get to safety."

Jack grabbed a potion of invisibility from his inventory and handed it to Toby. The two drank the potion and followed Harriet out of the mineshaft and into the night. They sprinted through the dark, and as they reached the jungle, their skins began to become visible.

"I can see you guys." Jack stopped to catch his breath.

"And we can see you," replied Harriet.

Jack spotted two Endermen walking toward them. "I think we should build a place to stay for the night. Quickly."

Toby and Harriet agreed, and the group quickly constructed a crude structure to spend the night in, narrowly avoiding attack from the two Endermen carrying blocks. Once they were safely in their beds, Harriet started to think about the journal again. "Do you really believe reading the journal will lead us to William the Explorer?"

"Imagine if we find him. We'll be famous!" exclaimed Jack.

"That's not the reason to find him. If he's missing, he might be in trouble—we could try to help him," said Harriet.

"I think we should follow the journal and retrace his steps. I bet that will lead us to him," said Toby.

"Wow, tracing the steps of the famed explorer. That does sound like fun," said Harriet. "*And* we might be able to help him. Let's do it!"

"I'll read the next journal entry aloud, and we can try to figure out where he was in the Overworld," said Toby. "Then we'll plot our trip." Toby took the tattered journal from his inventory.

But Jack was having doubts about reading from the journal again. "We've encountered a lot of hostile mobs since we started reading. Do you think we might actually be cursed?"

Toby was annoyed. "I told you there is no way you can be cursed from reading a book!"

A gasp came from Harriet as someone ripped the door from the hinge. "Who's out there?"

"Oh no!" cried Jack. "More zombies!"

The gang jumped out of bed, put on their diamond armor, and began to battle the zombies in front of their small house. It was a quick battle, but they were going to have to do something about that door.

Harriet looked through her inventory for supplies to rebuild the portion of the house that had been destroyed in the attack. "I could use some help here!" she said.

When the door was complete, they all climbed back into their beds.

"Should we continue with our bedtime story?" Toby joked.

Harriet hesitated. "Maybe Jack was right and we shouldn't read the journal after all."

"I've changed my mind—I don't care if we're cursed, I want to hear the rest." Jack was feeling bold after the battle and eager to hear the next chapter.

"But what if more hostile mobs spawn as Toby starts to read?" asked Harriet.

"The zombies have nothing to do with the journal," said Toby, and he picked up the book.

But before he could start reading, Jack interrupted. "Do you think Charles and Thao had something to do with William's disappearance?"

"Have you ever heard of Charles and Thao?" asked Harriet.

"No. When we studied the great explorers of the Overworld, I don't remember hearing about them at all," Jack replied.

"Don't you find that strange? If they were the noted explorers before William, why wouldn't we have heard about them?" Harriet wondered.

"I don't know, but you're right—that is very strange," Jack agreed.

"There's only one way we'll find out." Toby looked at the journal. "Should I start reading again?"

Harriet looked at the door. She crawled out of bed and opened it. There were no hostile mobs in sight. She lit a torch and placed it by the entrance of the building. "Okay, go ahead. Read," she said as she walked back into the house and snuggled down into the comfort of the bed.

4

JOURNAL ENTRY: MY FRIEND OLIVER

Trip 2: Explorations in the Desert

Oliver and I had read about the desert for a very long time before we finally made it to that region of the Overworld. Nothing prepared us for the trip. Almost as soon as we reached the desert, Oliver stumbled upon a desert temple. Oliver is a naturally curious person, but he has a dangerous tendency to be overly trusting. He trusts a lot of people who don't deserve his trust. I, on the other hand, trust no one. Oliver finds this rather appalling and has expressed this on numerous occasions.

When we reached the entrance of the ornate and spacious desert temple, a man wearing a black helmet approached Oliver.

"Who are you?" the man asked Oliver.

Before Oliver could respond, I intervened and said, "Why do you want to know?"

"Because this is my temple," the man in the black helmet declared.

I knew the man wasn't telling the truth. Desert temples spawn naturally in the desert and don't have owners. We had the same right to enter that temple as the man in the black helmet.

I told him as much. "Everyone is allowed in these temples. Please move out of the way so we may enter."

The man took out his sword. "No. You won't be entering without giving me at least five diamonds."

I noticed Oliver checking his inventory. Before he got cheated of his treasure, I jumped in. "We don't have diamonds. I'm sorry, but we'd still like to enter."

"That's impossible," the man replied.

"Now that's just not true," I said to the man. But before we could get into a proper debate about the temple, the man summoned an army.

A large group of men dressed in blue emerged from the desert temple and attacked us with swords, arrows, and potions. In a matter of seconds, we had very few hearts left, and I knew we'd respawn if we didn't stop them quickly.

"We surrender!" I shouted. "I'll give you the diamonds!"

The man in the black helmet ordered his men to stop. "Follow me," he said with a laugh.

We followed him into the desert temple. Although I questioned his motives, exploring the temple was amazing. I had dreamt about unearthing treasure in the temple, but I knew they had already looted the property.

The man was leading us deeper and deeper into the temple. "Where are we going?" I asked.

"You'll find out soon," he replied with another laugh. This time it sounded more sinister.

My heart sunk when I saw the jail cell. We had walked right into a trap. We had been so excited to become explorers and now we were probably going to spend the rest of our lives trapped in a basement prison in a desert temple. We would be prisoners. This wasn't the amazing journey I had imagined. I wasn't just disappointed—I was devastated.

This was the last opportunity for me to use my wits and stage an escape. Before he put us into that cell, I needed to act quickly.

The man in the black helmet was distracted, arguing with two of his men about something to do with the security of the cell. When he wasn't looking, I grabbed a golden apple from my inventory and ate it quietly. Then I snuck another to Oliver. Once our energy was restored, I swung out my sword and lunged at the man in the black helmet. Oliver joined me in battle, and with a few blows, we had destroyed the man in the black helmet. The two guards fled.

"How are we going to escape?" Oliver asked. "I'm sure the rest of his army will be here soon."

I splashed a potion of invisibility on us, and we sprinted toward the exit. We both stopped when we reached the door. Charles and Thao were standing in front of us, instructing the army to search the temple.

The man in black wasn't working on his own.

"We need to find those two so-called explorers and destroy them!" Charles ordered the army.

The men in blue took off in every direction. They were hunting for us. Oliver and I started running to get as far away from the desert temple as we could. When we were safely by the shore, we slowed down and eventually become visible again. "We have made some serious enemies," I announced.

"What are we going to do?" Oliver was worried. "Maybe we should go home after all."

"My dear Oliver, we don't just give up because someone tells us we can't do something. That isn't the way anything gets done. We want to explore the Overworld and create a guide for the people of the Overworld, and nobody is going to stop us."

"But we might be destroyed by Charles and Thao."

"That's a risk we'll have to take."

"Maybe we should just let Charles and Thao be the only explorers in the Overworld."

"Oliver," I said, "Charles and Thao have done nothing to help the Overworld. They don't share their maps—all they do is loot temples and bask in the glory of their adventures. They're greedy, and they're in this for the fortune and fame. We can map the Overworld and share that information—help pave the way so others can explore the Overworld too." We couldn't give up.

"Well," said Oliver, "then where should we go next?"

"I bet they'll never think to look for us in the cold biome," I suggested.

"You're right! They'll never think we'd go back there."

Oliver and I hurried back to the cold biome, and climbed up the mountain for a third time. I was still taken by the view of our town. The longer we spent away from home, the more I missed it.

We crossed over to the ice biome and we marveled at the fresh snow.

"Let's craft some snowballs. You never know when we'll need them." I grabbed some snow from beside me.

Oliver started to gather his own snow, and then I heard him shout, "Oh no!"

Without turning around, I asked, "Oliver? What's the matter?"

He didn't reply. I turned around, and there were Charles and Thao, standing right in front of us. They had their swords pointed directly at us. I threw a snowball, but I shouldn't have wasted the ammo. The entire army was right behind them. We were outnumbered.

5
MAPS AND SNOWBALLS

s Toby finished the second entry, a loud *boom* crashed from outside the house.

Harriet wanted to pull the blankets over her head and ignore the explosion. Hadn't they done enough fighting for today? But she couldn't. Jack and Toby ran out the door to search for the source of the explosion, and she pulled herself out of bed.

"Watch out!" she cried as she reached the door. A spider jockey had jumped out from behind a tree; the skeleton shot an arrow at Jack.

Harriet slowly aimed her bow and arrow at the attacking spider jockey. "Bulls-eye!" she called out. But despite her great shot, the skeleton was still coming toward them.

Jack splashed a potion on the skeleton, while Toby charged at the vicious mob with his diamond sword. Toby struck the red-eyed spider, as Harriet's next arrow destroyed the skeleton for good.

"Help!" a voice called out.

Harriet moved toward the sound of the voice. "I think someone is in the smoke!" she shouted.

Toby plunged his sword into the spider, finally destroying it, too. "What are we going to do?"

"I'm going to find them!" Harriet sprinted in the direction of the recent explosion.

A man stood in front of a large hole. "Someone blew up my house!"

"That's awful." Harriet studied the remains of the burnt home.

"I was fighting off zombies. When I turned around to go back home, it exploded," the man told them.

"Do you have any enemies?" asked Jack.

"Not that I know of. I live alone and lead a very quiet life."

"You can stay at our house tonight," said Harriet. "We can make an extra bed for you."

The man was extremely grateful. "Thank you. You're so kind."

Almost immediately, Harriet regretted offering the man a place to stay. She thought about the journal entry they had just read. William believed Oliver was too trusting. Maybe she was like Oliver. She didn't know this man and he could be a griefer.

While she crafted the bed, Harriet asked the stranger some questions. She wanted to know more about the man she had invited into their home.

"Who are you?" she asked. "What's your name? Where did you come from?"

"My name is Julian," he said. "I'm a farmer. I've lived in this part of the Overworld my entire life. I don't like exploring. You guys must be new here—I've never seen you before."

"Yes, we're just here for the night," explained Harriet.

They all crawled into bed. Harriet had a hard time falling asleep. She was worried Julian was going to steal from them. When morning came, she woke and looked over at Julian's bed. "It's empty!"

"What?" Jack asked as he woke up.

"Julian left," she announced.

"Maybe we should check if he took any of our stuff." Toby looked through his inventory. "Wait, I can't find the journal."

"What?" Harriet panicked. "He stole the journal!"

Jack searched the house, and crawled underneath the beds. "No, it's here. He didn't take it." He handed the book to Toby, who placed it safely in his inventory.

"We have to be more careful with this," said Toby. "We can't let it out of our sight."

Harriet let out a loud sigh of relief. "I'm so glad he didn't take it."

"But I still wonder where he went. He doesn't even have a house," said Toby.

"And he said he doesn't like to travel," added Jack.

"I guess it's going to have to be a mystery—he isn't important," said Toby. "We should head to the cold biome to retrace William's steps."

The gang filled up on breakfast food and left the small house. They walked past Julian's farm, but didn't see him.

"I wonder where he is," Harriet mused as they looked across the wheat farm. A small ocelot meowed and rubbed up against her feet.

"Let's get going," said Jack. "We want to get to the cold biome before dark."

"Maybe we can build an igloo once we're there," suggested Toby.

The group trekked toward the cold biome and walked up a large mountain. Harriet paused at the top of the mountain. "I wonder if we could spot William's town from up here."

Jack searched the landscape, looking for signs of life. "I feel just like William and Oliver. It is beautiful up here."

Toby stared at the icy biome that was on the other side of the mountain. "I can't wait to slide on the ice. It looks like so much fun. And I want to have a snowball fight."

"We don't have time for silly games," scolded Harriet. "We're here to find William."

The gang made their way down the steep mountain, toward the ice biome. They passed an unusually high patch of snow and Harriet was the first to go over to check it out.

Toby took out a shovel and began to dig. "I'm looking for treasure," he joked, but he did think the patch of snow seemed out of place and was wondering if someone might have buried something beneath it. After unearthing the journal, he was curious about what other things they could find in the Overworld.

Harriet joined Toby. "Let's place a hopper here for the snow to collect in." She set one up right next to them. Jack started digging, too.

"I see something," Toby shouted to the others.

"What is it?" asked Jack.

"I think it's a chest," said Toby.

"Open it!" Jack and Harriet stood next to him, waiting.

Toby opened the chest. "Blue helmets. It's filled with blue helmets!"

"Huh," said Jack.

"Blue helmets!" exclaimed Harriet. "They must have belonged to the blue army that was terrorizing William and Oliver."

"That means we're in the right place. This is the same ice biome where William was exploring." Jack was excited.

"We're one step closer to finding him." Harriet grinned.

"Let's keep digging and see if we find anything else," suggested Toby.

Everyone took out their shovels and dug deep into the cold, white snow. Toby shouted, "I see a door!"

The others dug as quickly as they could until they were able to crawl into the hole to get to the door. Jack opened the door slowly. "There's a staircase inside."

Harriet hadn't followed the others to the door. Toby called back, "What's wrong?"

Harriet hesitated. "Maybe we should read the next section of the journal before we go down that staircase. It might help us."

"You might be right," said Toby. "We might be walking right into a trap."

He started to read from the third journal entry.

6
JOURNAL ENTRY: SECRET ARMIES

Trip 3: Ice Age

We surrendered.

"You win!" I shouted.

"We knew we would." Charles grimaced.

Charles and Thao marched us through the ice biome and into a snow-covered cave. Deep in the cave was a small, dark jail cell. Charles laughed as he opened the door to the cell. "Here's your new home." He pushed us inside, then closed the door and left. I heard a key turn in the lock. "Good luck escaping this time."

Oliver was very anxious. "What are we going to do? How are we going to escape?"

"I'm not sure," I admitted, "but we'll try our best to come up with a plan. At least he didn't empty our inventories. Do you happen to have a shovel?"

Oliver searched his inventory. "I only have one "

"I guess I'll use a pickaxe." I grabbed one from my own inventory and began to dig a hole in the snowy floor. "We'll dig our way out of here."

Oliver and I dug for a while. We were lucky that nobody came to check on us. I assumed they weren't worried about us just then. Of course, once they discovered we were missing, we'd become a lot more important.

I climbed into the hole and Oliver followed. We were able to make a tunnel and escape. As we climbed out of the hole, Oliver spotted two blue men. We ducked back down and waited until they passed, then sprinted out of the tunnel and to some nearby cover.

"How are we going to explore the Overworld with this army chasing us? We should just head back home." Oliver was exhausted. This wasn't the trip he had planned. He wanted to make maps of the Overworld, not fight an army led by two rival explorers. He wasn't a fighter like I was.

But I had to agree. I didn't want to give up, but there was no way we were going to get anywhere on our explorations with so many obstacles. We were about to leave the ice biome when three of the blue army men passed by us. This time there was nowhere to hide.

"Stop!" one of the blue men called out.

Oliver and I stood still, but our hearts were racing.

A blue soldier took out his sword. "We don't want to attack you—we just want to talk!"

"Then why do you have your sword out?" I asked the soldier.

"To make sure you don't escape," the third soldier explained.

The blue solider with the sword began to speak. "We don't want to work for Charles and Thao anymore. We aren't soldiers—we're prisoners. They took over our town and forced us to fight. They've felt threatened ever since they found out that you two want to become explorers."

I was stunned. I couldn't believe Charles and Thao had created an entire army just to stop us from exploring the Overworld. Of course ever-trusting Oliver blurted out, "We will help you. We were just about to go home and give up. But we'd rather help you overthrow Charles and Thao so that we can explore."

I was annoyed at Oliver. He didn't have to tell them everything. "Do you have names?" I asked them.

"Yes, I'm Roger," said the blue soldier with the sword.

Before the others could reply, I said, "If you want to work with us, you need to change your skins."

Roger dismissed my demand. "If we change our skins, they'll know we aren't in their army and will destroy us. If we keep our blue skins, it will be easier for us to stage an inside attack."

I was still a little wary, but I liked the idea of an inside attack and a secret army. I also knew we had to get far away from the ice biome or we'd be vulnerable to an attack ourselves.

The sky grew dark, and Oliver and I needed a place to stay. The blue soldiers walked us over to a patch of snow. They took out shovels and began to dig.

Before we could ask what they were doing, Roger said, "Look," and pointed into the large hole they'd created in the snow.

We looked down the hole and saw a door.

"This is where you'll stay. It's a secret room we built. We've been plotting to destroy Charles and Thao, and this room is where we have our meetings. It's quiet and it's safe."

Oliver immediately jumped into the hole and opened the door. I stopped for a moment. I wasn't sure if this was a trap.

The blue soldiers looked at me. "Aren't you going to join us?" asked Roger.

"You first," I said. The three blue men made their way down the hole ahead of me.

I had to take a chance. I climbed in after them and walked down the stairs. The room was surprisingly large and there was a second smaller room off of it full of beds.

"We should all get some sleep, so if we get destroyed, we know we'll respawn here." Roger climbed into a bed.

I took out my journal and tried to write beneath the covers. I didn't want anyone to see me writing—this journal must stay a secret. As the night set in, we all went to sleep. When we awoke, Roger and his friends were in the room debating ways to overthrow Charles and Thao.

Roger stood by a large chest. I walked over and peeked into it. It was filled with blue helmets.

"What are these for?" I asked.

"We took these from Charles and Thao. We were trying to see if we could find others to join our cause and be a part of this secret army," explained Roger.

At that moment, I considered putting on a blue skin and helmet and joining the secret army. But something in my heart told me that something wasn't right.

"Should we help you come up with a plan of attack?" asked Oliver.

I continued to explore the room, peeking into the two other chests that were on the floor.

Roger looked alarmed. "What are you doing? Those are our private chests. Don't open them!"

The other two soldiers aimed their bows and arrows at us.

"What did we do wrong?" Oliver asked the soldiers.

"Nothing!" I shouted.

"I disagree," said Roger. Now he was pointing his diamond sword at us, too.

I looked in the direction of the exit and tried to figure out a way to escape. I looked over at Oliver and whispered, "Use your potions."

7

CLIMBING A MOUNTAIN

They were interrupted when a familiar voice called out.

"Julian?" called back Harriet.

"Hi," said Julian. "I'm sorry—I followed you."

"Why?" Harriet looked down at the open door. She wanted to hide their discovery from him, but it was too late. "What happened? Why did you disappear?"

"I got scared. But I have no home. When I saw you guys walking by my farm, I called out to you, but you didn't turn around. So I decided to follow you."

"We didn't hear you," Harriet replied. She didn't remember hearing anyone call out their name and she didn't recall seeing Julian when they climbed up the mountain. She was skeptical, but couldn't help but be a little impressed that he had made the journey on his own.

Julian peeked down the hole. "What's that?"

"It's a stronghold. We think it's a secret room where an army used to be housed," said Jack.

Harriet was annoyed at Jack. She didn't want Julian to know about the room. He was too trusting—just like Oliver.

"What makes you think that?" asked Julian.

Jack paused. He saw Harriet shoot him a dirty look, and he knew he had said too much. "I don't know. A wild guess."

"That's a pretty wild guess," Julian said.

Night began to set in. The group crawled into the hole, and Julian followed them.

"Excuse me," Harriet called back. "Who said you could come with us?"

Julian paused. "I think you should be nicer to me—you might find me helpful."

Harriet didn't know what that meant. But she decided to leave it alone and let him follow them. Together they entered the secret room that was once used by the blue army. It was just as William had described in his journal. Harriet was in awe. She felt as if she was walking into the pages of a storybook as she inspected the room.

Before they could explore the room, Jack suggested they get some sleep. "We want to get rest and avoid hostile mobs." They walked into the smaller room and quickly fell asleep in the beds. When they awoke, they were ready to explore.

"I found a chest!" Toby shouted.

"What's in it?" Jack asked.

The group joined Toby and watched as he slowly opened the chest. It was filled with blue helmets. Toby sifted through them. "I think there's something hidden in the bottom."

"What?" Jack helped Toby remove the helmets to search the chest more carefully.

"It looks like it's a book." Toby pushed the helmets out of the way and grabbed the book from the bottom.

Harriet leaned over Toby and read the cover. "It's another of William's journals!"

Julian looked upset. "How do *you* know William?"

"Everyone knows William the Explorer. He was a famed explorer who went missing."

"Are you looking for him?" asked Julian.

"Yes," replied Toby. Harriet glared at him.

"Well, you're not going to find him," Julian said with a shaky voice.

"How do you know?" Harriet reached for her diamond sword. She didn't trust Julian.

"He was trapped a long time ago," explained Julian. "I don't even know if he still exists. He used to have this friend who always traveled with him. He was the first one they captured."

"Who captured them?" Harriet took out her sword and aimed it at Julian. "How do you know all of this?"

"I used to be a part of William's secret army," Julian confessed. "It was run by my friend Roger."

"You must be one of the blue soldiers from the journal," Toby let slip. Harriet stomped her foot. He wasn't taking a hint!

Julian was shocked. "You have another journal?"

"Yes, we do. But since you were there, you could probably tell us more than the journal," said Toby. "Can you tell us why your army turned against William and Oliver in this very room?"

"We were following orders from Roger. After that happened, I was scared and ran off to live on the wheat farm. It's hard to explain my past. I've been trying to forget it."

Harriet looked at Julian. "You acted as if you never left your town." She put down her sword. "Why did you really follow us here? How can you help us? Do you know where Charles and Thao are now?"

"I'm afraid I don't know much, but I'd like to help you find out more. This has been bothering me for a very long time. I want to find William and his friend."

Harriet looked around the room. "I think we have to search for clues. This is the best place to start. And we have to keep reading the journal. It's the only way we can get answers. Obviously, William was able to leave his first journal in an abandoned mineshaft after he was here, so we know he had to escape from here at some point."

"That's not true," said Toby. "Someone could have found it here and brought it to the mineshaft."

Everyone had a theory, but nobody knew where William was hiding. Or being hidden. Julian interrupted. "We'll find him. It's been my mission to help him, ever since I left him. I failed him when I left."

The group searched the two rooms. Harriet looked at the bed where William had slept and secretly written in his journal. She spotted another chest by the bed, and opened it.

"Guys, come quick," she called out.

Jack shouted, "Diamond armor!"

"I wonder if this belonged to William and Oliver," Harriet said. "Julian, do you know?" She turned to Julian, but he was no longer in the room.

"Julian?" Toby called out.

There was no response.

"He's gone," replied Jack. "Again."

"Seriously?" asked Harriet. They searched the rooms.

"And the door is closed!" Jack said, as he stood on the stairs. He banged on the door. "It's blocked!"

Toby rushed to the chest that contained the second journal. "He took William's journal!"

"I knew he wasn't to be trusted!" Harriet cried.

"What are we going to do?" Jack banged on the door with his pickaxe, but it stuck. "We're trapped!"

Toby took out William's original journal from his inventory. "We're going to read."

8
JOURNAL ENTRY: POTENT POTIONS

Trip 4: Journey to the Nether

Oliver had froze.

"Oliver," I whispered again, "use your potions."

Oliver grabbed a potion of weakness and splashed it onto Roger and his minions.

"Another!" I cried out.

Oliver splashed a potion of harming on them.

"Run!" I shouted.

We sprinted up the stairs. When we were almost out of the ice biome, Oliver stopped and said, "I think we should grab some snowballs. I have some bad news."

"What?" I asked as I started to craft snowballs and placed them in my inventory.

"We are running low on resources. I need to travel to the Nether."

My heart sunk. I'm a warrior, but I don't like being in the Nether. It's the one place where I feel really vulnerable. More than anything, I'm afraid of fire.

"I know you're afraid of fire," said Oliver, "but I do have some fire-resistant potions that we can use." He stepped back and crafted a portal.

Purple mist rose through the sky. As I passed through the portal and stood next to Oliver, I could see Roger and the blue soldiers running toward us. We disappeared into the Nether before they could reach us.

"Destroy it!" I ordered Oliver.

Oliver broke the portal quickly. "Now we don't have to worry about Roger and the blue men."

Two ghasts flew toward us, and I began to shake as one shot a fireball in my direction.

"Use the snowball," Oliver shouted.

I threw the snowball at the fiery beast and destroyed it. Oliver threw snowballs at the second ghast, obliterating it.

"This is going to be harder than we thought." I looked over at Oliver. He was trying to craft a map of the Nether. "We don't have time to craft maps—this is a matter of survival. Any minute now we'll be confronted by Roger and his army of two, and they are going to be mad."

Oliver told me to calm down. "We'll be fine. I think making this map will help us, too. We'll want to know where we've traveled."

"Where can you find the supplies for brewing?"

Oliver smiled. "The Nether fortress—I see one up ahead."

I looked out into the distance. Although I dislike fire, there was something beautiful about the Nether. The netherrack ground seemed to omit a glow, and the lava waterfalls mesmerized me. The Nether fortress was very large and stood out from the landscape.

"It doesn't look that far. I think we should run," I suggested to Oliver.

Oliver reminded me that we were running low on energy. "This will help us." He handed me a potion and I took a sip.

Oliver was right. I felt strong again and I sprinted toward the Nether fortress. However, once we reached the entrance, I let out a loud gasp. Three blazes flew above the entrance. The yellow beasts with menacing black eyes shot fireballs at us.

Oliver grabbed a snowball and threw it at a blaze, while I shot an arrow. We destroyed one of them almost immediately. "William, pick up the glowstone dust," shouted Oliver. "I need it for my supplies. The dust helps make my potions stronger."

I nervously picked up the dust as I tried to avoid being struck by one of the fireballs the remaining blazes were shooting at us. Oliver struck another with a snowball, and the weakened mob was destroyed. I picked up the glowstone dust it dropped as Oliver annihilated the final blaze.

"Thanks for getting the glowstone dust," said Oliver. "It'll definitely come in handy."

We walked under a bridge made of Nether bricks, and were about to enter the fortress when lightning lit up the Nether sky.

"Lightning! There is never lightning in the Nether. This must be Roger's work. He must be summoning it." I knew this was going to be a hard battle to win. I hated being in the Nether.

"Yes! He also summoned creepers!" Oliver shouted.

Two creepers silently moved through the Nether landscape and were struck by the lightning. The charged creepers crept toward us and entered the fortress. Oliver and I aimed our bows and arrows at the creepers, but we put our weapons down when we noticed two wither skeletons spawn in the fortress.

Kaboom!

The charged creepers exploded and destroyed the wither skeletons. The black skeletons' skulls dropped to the ground. Oliver rushed to pick them up. "These are very valuable," he noted.

"We need to make this quick," I told him. I was worried Roger would summon more mobs and lightning.

We entered the main room of the fortress. Oliver walked over to a patch of soul sand and gathered Nether wart.

"I have everything we need. We can leave now," he said.

"Shh!" I whispered. "I hear voices."

As we stood in silence, two more wither skeletons spawned in front of us. I grabbed my sword and struck one. Oliver shot an arrow at the other skeleton. The powerful skeletons struck us, and we lost hearts.

"What's going on here?" Roger joined our battle with the wither skeletons. "I thought the creepers would have destroyed you by now."

I delivered a final blow to one of the skeletons and it was destroyed. Oliver was weakening the other skeleton, but not quickly enough. Roger was shooting arrows at us, too, now. My energy was almost entirely depleted. I used the last bit I had to run at the skeleton and plunged my sword into the beast of the Nether, obliterating it for once and for all.

Oliver splashed a potion of harming on Roger and the two blue soldiers to slow them down, and we sprinted out of the Nether fortress.

"We have to make a portal." I could barely get the words out, I was breathing so fast.

"I know, but we have to get away from Roger and the others first," Oliver said.

I looked back. Two ghasts were flying toward Roger and his friends. They shot fireballs at them. I stopped.

"Why are you stopping?" Oliver asked.

"Look—the ghast just hit Roger with a fireball," I pointed out. We watched the two soldiers attempt to battle the ghasts. They threw snowballs, but they lost to the fiery mobs. Within seconds Roger's two-person army was destroyed.

"Now we are safe to build the portal," I said. Oliver began to craft the portal back to the Overworld.

As the purple mist rose through the air, I stepped through the portal, but heard a voice call out in the distance, "Wait for me!"

9
BREWING

Who was calling to them? Keep reading!" said Harriet.

"No, this isn't helping. I thought reading the journal was going to help us figure a way out of here, but it's done nothing for us. I truly believe this book has cursed us." Jack paced around the small room.

"I told you, there is no such thing as being cursed." Toby looked through his inventory. "Does anyone have TNT? We're going to have to blow up the door."

"We can't blow up the door! We'll be destroyed," cried Jack.

"We're trapped. How did we let this happen?" asked Harriet.

"I'm sure we can find a way to blow up this door with TNT and not get destroyed in the process. Go into the other room." Toby grabbed a brick of TNT from Jack and placed it by the door. He ignited the TNT and then sprinted back toward the room with the beds.

Kaboom!

The door was blown apart and the trio made their escape out of the ice biome and toward the mountain.

"I don't think we should retrace their steps to the Nether," Jack called out as they climbed up the side of the mountain.

"I agree with you." Harriet disliked the Nether almost as much as William. "They were in a rush to get out of there anyway. They probably didn't leave any clues there."

When they climbed down the other side of the mountain, they reached a grassy biome.

"It's so peaceful here," Harriet said, but the minute those words fell from her mouth, the sky grew dark and it began to rain.

The group looked for a place to get shelter from the rain, but there was nowhere to hide.

Skeletons began to spawn in the fields. The gang prepared to battle the bony beasts until the rain stopped.

"We are cursed," Harriet said sadly.

"We can't give up. We're going to save William and Oliver." Toby shot an arrow at a skeleton.

Jack ran toward the skeletons and struck as many as he could with his diamond sword.

"More are spawning," Toby shouted as he splashed potions on them.

Harriet struck a skeleton with her sword and destroyed it. As she reached over to pick up the bone the skeleton had dropped, another skeleton struck her, and she was destroyed.

Exhausted, Harriet respawned in the blue army's secret room with the beds. She could hear voices in the other room. She kept quiet, not wanting to alert anyone to her presence. She listened.

"They blew up the door," she heard Julian say in the other room.

"Wow, they're resourceful," a second person replied.

"I really thought I'd be able to keep them here for a little while. I wanted them to meet you." Julian spoke again to the unknown person.

Harriet wanted to see who was there, but she didn't want to get trapped in the room. She waited for the others to respawn, hoping she'd have backup soon. Meanwhile, she continued to eavesdrop.

"I was able to save the second journal. I don't think it's a good idea that they read it."

"You did a good job, Julian," the man said. "I want to thank you for all your effort. But the job isn't done. I need to meet with these new explorers. And I need the first journal. The longer they have it in their hands, the stronger the curse will become."

Harriet's heart skipped a beat. She wondered if they could really be cursed. But she still wanted to finish reading the journal.

"I will get the journal from them and I will lead you them to you," Julian told the man.

"Thank you, Julian. You're a good friend."

"I'll admit, I don't know where they are, but I'll search the entire Overworld until I find them. I promise."

"Julian, I know you're a loyal friend," the man replied.

Harriet heard Julian and the man leave the room. They walked up the stairs. She tried to catch a glimpse of them on their way out, but she was too late. When they had been gone for a while, Harriet walked into the room to search for clues. Maybe they had left something behind that would help her identify the man who had been with Julian.

"Harriet?" a voice called out from the other room.

"Who's there?" Harriet asked nervously.

"It's me. Jack."

"Where's Toby?"

"He's still battling the skeletons." Jack walked into the room.

Within seconds, Toby respawned. "Jack? Harriet?"

"We're here," Harriet called to him.

"That was an intense battle." Toby was exhausted. He grabbed a potion of healing and drank some. Then he offered it to the others.

Harriet took carrots from her inventory and shared them with the others. "We need to eat and get our energy up. I have a lot to tell you."

She told them about Julian and the stranger. And she told them about the journal actually being cursed.

Toby asked, "Really cursed? Could it really be?"

"I wonder who that person was with Julian," said Jack.

"I know this might sound naive, but I don't think Julian wanted to hurt us," said Harriet. "He just wanted to trap us so we could meet this man."

"Once we find out who he is, maybe this will all make sense," said Toby.

"And how are we going to do that?" Jack's voice shook as he asked the question.

"I don't know," said Harriet, "but he meant a lot to Julian. In fact, Julian promised him that he would search the entire Overworld to find us."

"Why? We're not that important," said Jack.

"No, we're not." Toby paused and then took William's journal from his inventory. "But this is. I don't think they want to find us; I believe they want to find this journal."

"I bet they think we read the entire thing, which means we know a lot of things we shouldn't," said Harriet.

"That's what makes us important." Jack gulped. "But I don't think that's a good thing."

"We're cursed!" Harriet cried.

"Stop." Toby looked at the book. "We need to read the rest. It's our only hope."

10
JOURNAL ENTRY: THE WHEAT FARM

Trip 5: Explorations on a Wheat Farm

Oliver and I were already covered in purple mist when the blue soldier jumped through our portal.

"Don't hurt us!" Oliver cried out.

"That's not my plan," the blue man replied.

Before we could utter another word, we were back in the Overworld.

The blue man quickly broke the portal. "I'm being followed."

"By Roger?" I asked.

"Yes," he replied. "I need help. I don't want to be a part of their army."

The portal had left us in the middle of a desert— there was sand everywhere. I spotted some water in the distance and what looked like a desert temple. It was different from the temple we had visited earlier.

"I think we should make our way toward the temple. Maybe there's treasure in there," I suggested.

Oliver began to craft a map. "This would be very valuable. People in the Overworld are always looking for desert temples. If I can lead them to the temple with my map, that would be fantastic."

The blue man said, "That's a good idea, but I'd like to change my skin first, if you don't mind."

"That's fine," I said, and then asked, "But who are you?"

"My name is Julian," the man said as he put on a new skin. He had dark hair and wore a gray shirt. "I never wanted to be a part of that army. I thought Roger was going to lead us to victory over Charles and Thao, but he is even worse than they are. He wanted to take over once he destroyed them."

"We'll help you escape," Oliver said.

Unlike Oliver, I was wary of Julian. Could we really trust him?

"Where do you want to escape to?" I asked Julian as we walked toward the desert temple.

"I'd like to go back to my wheat farm. I used to be a farmer."

"We'll help you get there," Oliver reassured him.

As we made our way through the sand toward the temple, Julian cried out. "Ouch!"

"It's Charles and Thao!" I shouted.

They stood beneath an arch near the desert temple and were shooting arrows at us. Their enormous army erupted from the desert temple and attacked. We didn't want to be taken prisoner, so we fled the desert as fast as we could move.

"Take this." Oliver handed us bottles of potion of invisibility, and quickly we were safely out of sight.

With nowhere else to go, we decided to take Julian home. When we reached Julian's village, he was happy, but it was a bittersweet return.

He explained: "The town isn't the same since Charles and Thao arrived. At first we were all excited for explorers to visit our town, but then they started recruiting people for the army. Nobody wanted to go, so they forced a group of us to join. The town was upset to see us go. I bet they'll be surprised to see me back."

Julian was right. The minute we walked through the small village, a librarian wearing a white robe called to him. "Julian!"

"Tess!" he shouted, running up to her.

"How did you escape?"

"It wasn't easy."

"What about the others?"

"I'm the only one I know who escaped. I just want to get back to my farm."

Julian led us to his wheat farm. There was a small house. An ocelot purred and rubbed up against his feet. "This is Snowball," he said, petting her gently.

We were exhausted—as we entered Julian's house, night was beginning to set in.

"I know you're happy to stay here on your farm," I said to Julian, "but we could use your help to stop Charles and Thao. Once they're defeated, we can become the explorers that we want to be, and then you can return to your wheat farm for good."

"But how are we going to defeat them? They have an army. They're so powerful."

"I have no idea," I told him. "Do you know any weaknesses they might have? You were in their army."

Oliver added, "Yes, we all have weaknesses. Maybe they're afraid of fire, like William."

I glared at him. Again, Oliver was too trusting. Now that Julian knew my weakness he could use that against us. I hoped he really was on our side.

Julian thought for a moment. "I know that Charles is very afraid of going to the End—I think it's because he's afraid of the Ender Dragon."

"Maybe we can summon Ender Dragons to attack them in the desert," I suggested.

"That's a good idea," said Oliver. "We can do that with command blocks."

"I think we should all get some sleep first," said Julian. "We can attack them in the morning."

As they both slept, I secretly wrote in my journal. As I write now, I am excited for our plan. I have never summoned an Ender Dragon before, and I think this attack on their desert headquarters might work. Then we'll finally be able to continue our lives as true explorers.

11

TRACKING DOWN OLD FRIENDS

So Julian isn't a bad guy?" asked Harriet.

"So far, he isn't, but I think we have to read more," said Toby.

"We should just go back the wheat farm and find Julian. I think he is a good guy, and hopefully he'll be able to give us some answers," suggested Jack.

"I want to get out of this ice biome, and I hate this secret room. I keep thinking we're going to get trapped again," Harriet said as she walked toward the door.

As the group made their way to Julian's town, Jack reminded them, "We still have a house there."

"Yes," said Harriet, "that is very helpful."

As they continued on, Toby mused, "I wonder if Julian's house exploding has to do with his past? Maybe the explosion has a link to Charles and Thao?"

"Yes, they could still be around and terrorizing him," said Harriet.

The town was bustling, and people walked through the streets, entering the shops. A librarian in a white robe walked by them, and Jack called out to her. "Are you Tess?"

"Yes." She was surprised. "How do you know my name?"

"We're friends with Julian," Jack replied.

"Julian," Tess paused. "Do you know where he is?"

"We thought Julian was here," said Harriet.

"No, Julian's house exploded a few nights ago, and he has been missing ever since. It's awful. Everyone is worried about him."

"Don't worry, we'll find him," Harriet told Tess.

"We'll search his farm for some clues," added Toby.

"That's wonderful," said Tess. "If you find him, can you please tell him to come see me? I've been very worried about him."

The gang told Tess they would do their best, and then walked on toward his home. When they reached the wheat farm, an ocelot meowed.

"That must be Snowball," Harriet remarked. She found him hiding and reached down to pet the ocelot. They walked around the farm inspecting it.

"I don't see any clues," said Jack, looking around carefully.

"Me neither," said Toby.

The sky grew dark. Harriet suggested they head to their house before night set in.

Before they reached the house, two Endermen walked by them. One of the Endermen stared at Harriet, let out a loud piercing shriek, and teleported right in front of her. She lashed out with her diamond sword, but the Enderman kept attacking. Jack approached the Enderman from behind and struck it with his diamond sword. With one final hit from Harriet, the Enderman was destroyed.

The second Enderman attacked Toby. Harriet and Jack ran to his side and helped him defeat the lanky mob. When the two Endermen were defeated, the trio returned to the house.

"Oh no!" Harriet cried.

"What happened to the house?" Jack shouted.

The house had been blown up. Just like Julian's. A cluster of endermites crawled around the ground beside the remnants of the building.

They used their diamond swords to battle the bugs. "We'll have to rebuild," said Harriet as she swung at one of the creatures.

Toby annihilated the final endermite and then looked through his inventory for supplies to craft a house. "I don't have any wood."

Jack and Harriet looked through their inventories. They didn't have any wood, either.

"What are we going to do?" Jack stared at the dark sky. "There's no way we'll survive the night without shelter."

The group walked back into town. They hoped somebody might offer them a place to stay. As they trekked through the quiet town, a voice called out to them.

"Who's there?" Harriet couldn't see anyone.

"It's me," the voice replied.

The group stood still and looked for the person who was calling to them, but they couldn't see anyone nearby.

"It's me—Julian." Julian walked into the center of the town.

"What are you doing here?" asked Harriet.

"Come with me," Julian told them. "Let me help you."

The group followed Julian out of the town and into a grassy biome. They could see zombies spawning just a few feet in front of them. Julian grabbed a potion and splashed it on the zombies.

"Where are you taking us?" Jack asked as he swung his diamond sword at the zombies.

"I can't tell you. But I want you to meet someone very important," Julian replied.

Harriet destroyed the final zombie. "We don't want to follow you unless we know where we are going."

Julian looked at the gang. "I'm sorry, but you're just going to have to trust me."

They glanced at one another and then followed Julian into the dark night and up a mountain. "Are you taking us to the ice biome?" asked Jack.

Julian replied, "I told you, I can't tell you where we are going, but I can tell you, it's very important that you come with me."

The group traveled all night as the sun began to rise. A chicken spawned in front of them. Julian hunted the chicken and offered the group some food. "We need to eat and replenish our energy. We are about to do something amazing."

Harriet accepted the piece of chicken, wondering what amazing thing they were going to do.

"I have to travel the rest of the journey on my own," said Julian, "and will meet you back here. But you have to promise to stay here and wait for me."

Harriet saw a stretch of beach up ahead. "We'll wait on that beach, but we'll only wait until dusk. We need to find a place to stay when it gets dark."

Julian promised he wouldn't be very long, and thanked them and left to continued on.

"So, we're just supposed to wait here?" Jack asked when Julian was out of earshot.

"I guess so," replied Harriet.

Toby took out the journal. "At least we can read this while Julian is away."

12

JOURNAL ENTRY:
DANGEROUS DESERT

Trip 6: The Ender Dragon War

I had never summoned anything with command blocks. Julian helped as we worked on summoning several Ender Dragons to spawn in the desert.

"How many should we spawn?" I asked.

"As many as we can," Julian replied.

We summoned four Ender Dragons and sprinted to the desert to watch our attack take place. Our plan was enter the outskirts of the desert, dig a hole into a dune and watch from there. We wanted to make sure we won, but we didn't want to have to fight. As we reached the sandy biome, Julian pointed to the winged beasts that flew overhead. We could hear Charles shout, "Oh no! Not the Ender Dragon!" We could hear the dragon let out a loud roar.

"There are more than one!" Thao shouted.

We couldn't see very much from inside the hole that we had built, but we heard an explosion, and then we heard Charles order his troops to start throwing snowballs. We waited until the sky began to grow dark.

"What are we going to do?" asked Oliver. "We need to find a place to spend the night."

Julian suggested that we keep digging and set up an underground bunker similar to the one they had in the ice biome. We both agreed that was a good idea and began to work on constructing it.

As we dug deeper, I noticed a door.

"What's that?" Oliver asked.

"We're in luck," Julian told us. "We've found a stronghold. We can probably craft beds in there."

I opened the door to the stronghold. The first room was very large and filled with silverfish. Oliver and I destroyed the silverfish, as Julian searched for the spawner.

"Found it!" he called out. A moment passed. "It's destroyed!" he shouted.

I couldn't concentrate. Even though there was a quiet room to craft beds, I wanted to know what was going on above us. I wished we had a periscope, like on a submarine, to see the battle between Charles, Thao, and the Ender Dragons.

When we awoke, I made my way to the exit, climbed to the top of the hole, and peeked out. There was nobody outside. A lone Ender Dragon flew through the sky, and the desert temple was partially destroyed.

"I think we won," I told the others.

We put on armor and went to explore the desert temple. It was eerily quiet. I entered the temple, readying myself for an attack, but it was abandoned. There was no sign of Charles, Thao, or their blue soldiers.

"This is fantastic!" Julian was thrilled that we had won the battle.

The Ender Dragon swept down and one of its scaly wings hit the side of the temple.

"I think we're going to have to destroy that Ender Dragon now," said Oliver.

Julian, Oliver, and I hurried outside and threw snowballs at the beast. It took about seven hits, but together we destroyed the dragon. It dropped an egg, and a portal to the End spawned by the desert temple. We chose not to travel to the End though. Not yet. We wanted to explore the temple.

Oliver spotted a large chest in one of the temple's many rooms. He opened it. "It's filled with diamonds."

"I've never seen that many diamonds," Julian marveled.

"I found another chest," Oliver called out. "And this one is filled with enchanted books."

We were about to distribute all of our newfound treasures, when I came up with another plan.

"This is a lot of stuff. I think it would be best if we bury it here and come back to get it later. Oliver and I are about to start our official exploration of the Overworld, and once we're done, we'll want these valuables."

Everyone agreed, and we began to bury the treasure deep inside the temple.

"I'm going back to my town to live on the wheat farm," said Julian. "When you're done with your first exploration, come find me, and we can travel back here and dig up the treasure together."

We said good-bye to Julian and began our first exploration. During the first few days of the exploration, we were convinced that Charles and Thao would return and stop us, but after a few weeks, we had almost forgotten about them. And after a few months, we felt safe enough to believe they wouldn't return. The Overworld was a happy place again, and everyone was able to live the lives they wanted. We kept exploring and made many discoveries.

Once Oliver had put together a collection of his maps, and I completed my notes, we began to present them to the people of the Overworld. The people were excited to hear about our adventures. They studied Oliver's maps and began to take their own journeys. The entire Overworld began to refer to our maps and notes, and we became a trusted source of information.

Whenever we traveled around the Overworld, people would treat us with respect. They were gracious and opened their homes to us when we visited a new town. People who wanted to hear about our explorations constantly surrounded us. It was an exciting time. It seemed as if we were always on the move, and visiting new towns. But although it had been a long time, we hadn't stopped by Julian's town.

We stopped at the top and I looked in the direction of his town in the landscape. I knew that would be our next trip.

13
SANDY DREAMS

We should try to find the treasure," Harriet said. "But we have to wait for Julian," Toby reminded us.

Jack looked up at the sky. "He told us he wouldn't be long, but look, the sun is going to set soon and we have no place to stay."

Harriet agreed. "We have to find shelter."

"If we go to the desert temple, I bet we can stay there. Then we can look for the treasure in the morning." Toby was excited. He loved a good treasure hunt.

"Let's just give Julian a few more minutes." Harriet looked out to see if Julian was approaching, but there was no sign of him.

The group waited a little while longer for Julian, but he didn't appear. "We have to go," said Jack. "It's getting dark."

They made their way to the sandy biome, running as fast as they could toward the desert. When they finally reached the desert, it was night.

Harriet spotted the desert temple in the distance. "There's the temple. We'll have to sprint there!"

Outside the desert temple were a few dead bushes and a couple of cacti. The desert temple was empty. The room that usually contained the treasure was looted, but they hoped the buried treasure still remained beneath the floor of the temple.

"We need to craft beds. We don't want to be exposed to hostile mobs," Toby warned the group.

The gang crafted their beds and then pulled the blue wool covers up and fell asleep. Harriet dreamt of the treasure they were going to dig the next morning. But she also wondered what had happened to Julian. She worried that he had been attacked. She tossed and turned, half awake. Eventually, she finally drifted off to sleep.

In the morning Jack woke them up. "I want to search for treasure."

The gang took their shovels and pickaxes and broke up away at the blocks. They dug deep into the surface, but they couldn't find anything.

"Do you think we're in the right temple?" Toby wondered.

"I think so," said Harriet. "It looks just like the one William described in the journal."

The gang spent the entire day digging holes in the temple. Night was beginning to set. They had just climbed into bed when they heard a noise. Harriet climbed back out to investigate.

She heard someone say, "Wait outside. I bet they're hiding in here."

The boys were right behind her. Jack took out his sword and approached the intruder, ready to attack.

"Stop!" the person called out.

"Julian?" Harriet was shocked.

"I had a feeling you'd be here," Julian told them.

"Why?" asked Harriet.

"Because you're reading the journal. I lived it, so I know what you're searching for, and you're not going to find it here. In fact, it's probably best if you end your journey here. Please let the past stay in the past. You are digging up old memories that should stay buried."

"But we want to find William and Oliver," said Harriet. "They could be hurt and in trouble."

"People have spent their entire lives searching for them," said Julian. "Just because you have an old journal doesn't mean you're going to find them."

Harriet wondered why Julian was so against their search for the missing explorers. And hadn't he said it was his mission to find them, himself? According to William's journal, they were friends. Wouldn't he want to find his friends?

Jack asked, "Who's outside?"

"I'll introduce you shortly. I just want you to promise that you won't look for William and Oliver. Just give up this search. The journals are too dangerous."

Toby paused. He thought about the journal and how far they had traveled to find William and Oliver. "I'm not sure we could do that. This is a mystery we really want to solve."

A man wearing a black helmet walked into the room.

"The man in the black helmet!" Toby shouted. "William and Oliver destroyed you."

"You were working with Charles and Thao," Harriet called out.

"That was a long time ago. I was like Julian. I was forced into working with them. They are long gone. As you know, William and Oliver destroyed them with their Ender Dragon attack."

"Why are you here? What do you want from us?" asked Harriet.

"I'm here to warn you about the journal. It's cursed. I've know people who have found it before, and they all suffered a terrible fate."

"We aren't going to give up," said Jack.

The man in the black helmet walked around the desert temple. Looking around, he said, "I see you've been searching for the buried treasure. You won't find it here."

"But we'll find it." Harriet said.

"Maybe. But you're searching in the wrong place," the man in the black helmet told them.

"So you know where it is?" questioned Harriet.

"No, I don't, but I know this temple is empty. There is nothing here but memories." The man in the black helmet looked down at the holes in the ground. "Don't you believe me? Look at the ground. The holes are empty."

Harriet was wary. She didn't trust the man in the black helmet. She looked over at Julian.

Julian confirmed it. "This temple is a sad place. I have bad memories here."

"All right," said Harriet. "I think we should go."

"Can I talk to you in private?" asked Toby.

Harriet, Jack, and Toby walked over to the corner and spoke in a hushed whisper.

"I have a feeling there is something here," whispered Toby. "I don't trust them, and they want us to leave so badly. I think that's a sign that we're onto something."

Jack agreed. "I bet there's a secret room here."

"But how are we going to explore the rest of the desert temple if they are here?" asked Harriet.

"Let's leave with them. We'll come back later on our own," said Jack.

The gang told Julian and the man in the black helmet that they were heading back home. Once they had traveled a bit further out of the desert, and when they were far enough away from Julian and the man in the black helmet, they constructed a house.

As they sat in their beds, they strategized a plan to explore the desert temple. "I bet there is a secret room," said Harriet.

"I know," said Jack. "They are definitely hiding something from us."

Toby opened the journal. "Maybe this will help." He began to read.

14

JOURNAL ENTRY: EXPLORATIONS AND FAME

Trip 7: Julian's Town

We had finally explored most of the Overworld and the Nether, and battled everything from zombies to ghasts, we were ready to see our old friend. I had promised him, and I try to never break my promises. The journey wasn't going to be easy. I stared at Oliver's map and realized that Julian's town was on the other side of the Overworld, and the journey would take quite awhile.

"I think it's time we visit Julian," I told Oliver.

"Good idea," Oliver said, studying the map.

I looked at the map again. "It looks like we'll have to travel through the swamp."

"Yes, and you don't like witches."

Despite being a warrior, witches scare me almost as much as fire, and I try to avoid them at any cost. So swamps are some of my least favorite places to go. But I had to see Julian, and there was no easy way to reach his village without traveling through the swamp biome.

"We could always teleport to Julian's town," suggested Oliver.

"That seems like cheating. We are world-renowned explorers. We don't TP."

"Well, then I think we should start our journey now." Oliver looked over at me.

"Yes, but let's go through our inventories and make sure we have all the supplies we need first."

We had well-stocked inventories. I took a sip of milk and a bite of a potato, and with that, we began our trip to Julian's village.

At first the journey seemed too easy. We traveled through grassy biomes, and the first night we built a shelter without any attacks from hostile mobs. But once we reached the swamp biome, I started feeling nervous.

"I don't see any witches." Oliver kept a close eye on the surroundings.

A bat flew close to my head. "I don't think that's necessarily a good sign. We know they're here some-where. . . ."

I was right. Within seconds, we came upon a small witch hut. A witch emerged from the house. She clutched a tiny bottle of potion in her hand.

"Watch out!" Oliver shouted.

I stood frozen in terror. I couldn't move. No matter how many times Oliver shouted warnings at me, I just couldn't. I was terrified. The witch was coming closer.

"William!" Oliver shouted. "Sprint!"

I wanted to run, but my legs wouldn't move. The witch was so close that I could have reached out and touched her—if I'd been able to move. She splashed a potion on me. Now I was frozen in place and I was weakened.

Oliver ran toward us. He lunged at the witch with his enchanted diamond sword and struck her before she had a chance to use another of her potions. With a few blows from the sword, she was destroyed. The witch dropped a glass bottle. Oliver leaned over and picked it up. He came over to me. "Drink this."

I sipped the potion Oliver handed me and regained my strength.

"You did a good job," Oliver told me.

"Me?" I laughed. "You were the one who destroyed the witch. I did nothing."

"You're still here, aren't you?" Oliver said, and we continued our journey to Julian's town.

When we entered Julian's town, crowds surrounded us. They were excited to meet the world-famous explorers. I don't want to sound like I'm bragging, but this happens to us whenever we enter a new town now. We've become celebrities.

Julian rushed over to us. "You guys finally came to visit! I've missed you!"

He introduced us to his friends. We saw Tess again and met many other villagers. He walked us over to the wheat farm and told us that he would throw a huge celebration for us that night. The townspeople were excited and everyone talked about the food they would bring to the big feast. Someone decided to plan a fireworks show, too. We were so happy. I was glad to see Julian and be reunited with my old friend.

While we dined on rabbit stew and baked potatoes, a townsperson named Hope asked me about the Nether. "Isn't it very dangerous and scary?"

"Not at all," I said, "if you know what you're doing. I can battle three ghasts without any hassle. And Oliver can battle a horde of blazes while still taking notes for his maps."

Oliver looked over at me. I could tell he was annoyed. I'll admit I was stretching the truth a little. But it didn't excuse Julian when he said, "William. Everyone knows you're afraid of fire."

I stared at him. Why would he reveal one of my biggest secrets? I didn't want anyone to know about my fears. To them, I was a fearless leader and explorer of the Overworld. I wanted it to stay that way.

"Me? Afraid of fire? You must be mistaking me with Oliver over there." I tried to laugh it off. I didn't want people to believe him.

The sky grew dark and people began to settle in for the fireworks show. As we watched the colorful display, I hoped that people had forgotten Julian's comment.

After the show, everyone headed home. We settled in Julian's house on the wheat farm. As we climbed into our beds, Julian suggested, "Tomorrow we should go look for the treasure we buried in the desert temple."

"Tomorrow, we are going to continue our explorations. We don't have time to go back to the desert and dig up that measly treasure," I replied.

"What? But that was our plan." Julian seemed very disappointed.

"Plans change," I said.

"People change." Julian was annoyed. Oliver was silent.

I fell asleep thinking about the treasure. Julian didn't deserve it. He had shared one of my secrets with the world. I didn't trust him.

15
FACT OR FICTION?

I think our answers are in that temple," said Harriet.

"Why?" Toby looked at the journal. "After reading this, I don't trust William. It seems like the fame has gone to his head."

"That doesn't make me not trust him. I get why he wouldn't want people knowing he was afraid of fire—that's personal," Harriet defended William.

Jack said, "Sometimes when you read the book I wonder what is fact and what is fiction. I mean this is how William sees everything, but it might not be the way things happened."

"Well, it is his journal." Toby stared at the tattered book.

"There's no point in debating this. I'm convinced that we'll get some answers at the desert temple. The treasure's missing and we need to find out who took it. Once we figure that out, I think we'll be closer to finding William and Oliver." Harriet was tired. She wanted to go to bed.

When the sun rose, Jack woke up the others and offered them some carrots. As the group ate breakfast, Jack asked, "Are we ready to head back to the desert temple today?"

"I think we should use the potion of invisibility," suggested Harriet. "I bet Julian and his friend are still lurking around the temple, and we don't want them to see us."

They all agreed. They made their way into the desert, and when they were close to the temple, they splashed the potion of invisibility on themselves.

They entered the temple carefully. It was eerily quiet. They searched the entire temple, but they couldn't find any secret room. The gang stopped when they heard voices. Harriet looked down at her hands "Oh no—it looks like the potion is wearing off."

They stood in the center of the desert temple and slowly began to reappear. Harriet gasped when she noticed Julian and his friend standing right in front of them.

"I knew you'd be back," he said.

"How could you know?" asked Jack.

"You remind me of William and Oliver. They were always very curious, and they were also very stubborn. You couldn't stop them from doing anything," said Julian.

"Which is why they wound up in trouble," the man in the black helmet added.

"I've spent my entire life searching for William and Oliver," said Julian. "That wasn't a lie. I miss my friends. And I don't know where they are. I'm worried about you reading the journals, but if you're not going to give up this quest, then maybe we should join forces."

Harriet, Toby, and Jack looked at one another. Harriet didn't trust Julian. This didn't feel sincere. The day before, he had been warning them not to search for William and Oliver, and now he wanted to join forces. She was confused.

"How can we help you?" she asked him.

"What information do you have from the journal?" He looked at the group. It was obvious he wasn't sure which person had the journal.

Harriet wondered if this was all a trick to get the journal from them. So she lied. "We lost it."

"Where?" asked Julian.

"We don't know for sure. In the cold biome, we think. It's also where we lost the second journal." Toby spoke fast and sounded nervous.

"I have the second journal," confessed Julian.

"You do?" Harriet was surprised that he was telling them.

"Yes. I didn't think you should have it. And I am still trying to figure out if it's a hoax. I don't remember William having a second journal," Julian replied.

"A hoax?" Harriet asked.

"I have my reasons for believing this, but I can't explain," said Julian.

"If we're supposed to work together, we have to tell each other everything we know. Otherwise this isn't going to work," said Harriet.

"Okay," Julian replied. "Do you still have the first journal?"

Harriet didn't like the direction this was going. She was still convinced that they were being tricked. Julian hadn't actually answered the question. "I think it's time we left. I want to explore. You're right. Searching for William and Oliver was a terrible idea, and it wasn't our original plan. We're done."

Jack and Toby followed Harriet out of the desert temple.

Julian called out after them. "Wait!"

He ran after the gang. They stopped and turned around. "What do you want?" asked Harriet. "We told you we weren't going to search for William and Oliver anymore. What more do you want from us?"

The man in the black helmet said, "We want your help."

"Why?" Jack asked.

For a minute there was utter silence. They just stood and stared at each other. Harriet could swear she heard a faint voice. It was muffled, but the voice sounded like it was calling for help. She didn't tell her friends; instead she just said, "Don't answer that question. We're done here."

They returned to the small house and climbed into bed. Before Toby began to read from the journal again, Harriet asked the others, "Did either of you hear someone calling for help when we were at the desert temple?"

"Yes!" Jack cried out. "I thought I was imagining it."

"Hey, me too!" said Toby.

"We have to go back tomorrow, but we can't let them have access to this journal."

Toby looked at the journal. Harriet and Jack went quiet as he read the next pages.

16
JOURNAL ENTRY: SECRET TEMPLE

Trip 8: Back to the Desert

I didn't want to go back to the desert. I didn't care about the treasure. I wanted to explore the Overworld, but I had promised Julian we could return, and Oliver was holding me to that promise. As we entered the temple, Julian began to pace.

"What's wrong?" I asked. "You seem nervous."

"I just want to find the treasure."

"We'll find it," I said, certain that we would.

But we didn't. We dug all over the temple and there was nothing there. Julian suggested that we had stolen it from him. And we blamed him for the missing treasure.

"I promise you," I said, "we didn't take the treasure."

"Then who did?" Julian was getting frustrated.

A man wearing a black helmet entered the desert temple and I took out my diamond sword. "Who are you?" I asked, pointing my sword at him.

"I'm Ezra," he said. "I know where your treasure is hidden."

"How?" I asked.

"Tell them who I am." He looked over at Julian.

"You know this man?" Oliver was shocked.

"Ezra used to be a part of the blue army." Julian spoke slowly. "But he stopped working with Charles and Thao."

"Where are Charles and Thao?" I asked.

"They're long gone," Ezra told us, "and we'll never have to worry about them again. When you staged the Ender Dragon attack, I used command blocks to switch them to Hardcore mode."

"Why would you betray them like that?" asked Oliver.

"I really didn't want to be a part of their army," replied Ezra. "They were terrible leaders."

"So then where is the treasure?" I asked.

"Well," said Ezra, "I know it isn't here."

"How could you know that?" Oliver asked.

"I live in the desert—I never left after the attack. And I once saw someone come into this temple and empty it," replied Ezra.

"Who?" asked Oliver.

"I'm not sure. I only caught a quick glimpse and I thought it was Charles, on his own. But I knew that was impossible. I had put him on Hardcore mode and he had been destroyed. There was no way he could come back."

"Maybe he knew you put him on Hardcore mode and stopped it?" I asked. I wasn't sure if I should trust Ezra.

I was also beginning to grow wary of Julian again. He had never told us about this friend from his blue army days. And what a coincidence for Ezra to suddenly appear in the desert temple while we were searching it. I felt like we were being tricked.

"I suppose that is a possibility," Ezra replied finally.

"Did you follow him?" asked Oliver.

"Yes, but I lost him," Ezra continued. "And then I thought I saw him here a few weeks ago. I tried to follow him again, but he noticed. He splashed a potion on himself and disappeared."

A roar was heard outside the desert temple. The wing from an Ender Dragon struck the side of the temple—almost immediately it crumbled.

"Watch out!" Oliver called out.

"Who summoned the Ender Dragon?" I shouted.

"It could be the mystery man. It could be Charles!" Ezra cried.

I grabbed all the snowballs I had in my inventory and tried to keep a brave face, but when the Ender Dragon let out a fiery breath, I was terrified. This is why we'd stayed so far away when we'd summoned the Ender Dragons the first time.

Oliver was at my side. He threw the first snowball at the dragon, but despite his good aim, one snowball didn't destroy the powerful creature.

Julian and Ezra joined in the battle. They hurled their own snowballs at the beast, but it was only weakening the dragon, not destroying it. And we were quickly losing energy.

"Who summoned this?" I asked aloud again, but realized I was talking to myself—everyone else was immersed in battle.

The dragon flew toward me, and instead of striking it with my sword, I sprinted back into the desert temple. I wanted to seek shelter from the horrid flying terror.

I was useless in battle. A warrior who couldn't fight.

I could hear them fighting from inside the temple. I felt terrible for abandoning my friends in battle, but I was no help. My fears had overtook me.

"I think I've got it!" I heard Julian call out as he slammed the fiery beast with the last of his snowball supply.

It went quiet outside. Then I heard Oliver. "William, where are you?"

As I came out of the temple, I spotted someone running by. It looked like Charles. "I think he's here!" I shouted.

Nobody was listening. They were all cheering for Julian, who had thrown the final snowball at the Ender Dragon. It had exploded, dropping a dragon egg and unleashing a portal to the End.

I joined them, but I couldn't see Oliver anywhere. "Where's Oliver?" I asked the others.

"He disappeared at the end of the battle," said Julian. "We aren't sure where he went."

"Sorry," said Ezra, "but we're going to the End. We don't want to miss this chance."

The two passed through the portal, leaving me to search for Oliver on my own. I looked around the temple, but he was nowhere in sight. First the treasure went missing and now my best friend was gone. We never should have come back. That's what I get for keeping my promise.

I spent the next day searching every block of the temple and all the land surrounding it. I couldn't find Oliver. I was starting to get nervous. I kind of missed him and I was worried he might have been taken prisoner. I hoped the person who looked like Charles would return and I could trap and question him. I wanted Oliver back. If my plan failed...well, there was nobody who could help me. I was all alone.

Kaboom!

I heard an explosion in the distance. I was shaking, but I went to explore the source of the noise. I had to find out if Oliver was somehow involved. It was getting dark, and two Endermen crept by. They were carrying blocks, and I tried not to make eye contact with them. The lanky Endermen didn't see me, but I knew it was just a matter of time before I was destroyed by one of the hostile mobs that spawned in the night. I was scared and I felt like a fraud. The entire Overworld celebrated me. They believed I was a fearless explorer. I had called myself a warrior. And here I was, friendless and scared. I missed Oliver.

17
PUZZLE PIECE

That's it," said Toby. "The rest of the pages are missing."

"We need to go back to the desert temple. I bet that voice we heard was Oliver," Harriet said.

She closed her eyes, but it was hard to sleep. There was so much to do tomorrow.

When they woke, the gang put on armor and made their way to the desert temple.

They stood in the temple and listened for the faint cry they had heard the day before, and they also kept an eye out for Julian and the man in the black helmet—Ezra.

They walked down the stairs and could hear the voice more clearly. "It sounds like the person is trapped in a room *underneath* the desert temple," said Harriet.

The gang got out their pickaxes and began to dig a hole on the bottom floor of the temple.

"Do you see anything?" asked Jack.

"Not yet," said Toby.

But then Harriet shouted out, "I found a stronghold!"

The group was about to open the door to the stronghold, when they heard a voice behind them.

"What did you find?"

Harriet whipped around and saw Julian standing by the wall.

"It looks like a stronghold," said Jack.

Harriet shot Jack a dirty look.

Ezra entered the desert temple. "Did you say a stronghold?"

"Yes." Jack looked down at the door. The sound of the voice called out again and this time it was much louder.

"Oliver, is that you?" shouted Julian.

"Julian!" the voice shouted gleefully. "Save me!"

Harriet, Toby, Jack, Julian, and Ezra stormed into the stronghold, and rushed to free Oliver.

They raced through a series of tunnels until they reached a door. Toby tried to open it.

"It's blocked." He looked at the others.

Oliver was calling from the other side of the door. "Break a hole in the wall. Do you have a pickaxe?"

The gang took out their pickaxes and began to break down the door and the wall. Oliver crawled through the hole. "Julian!"

They hugged. Julian was happy to see his old friend.

"Where's William?" Oliver looked at the group.

"We don't know," said Julian. "It took us years to find you. We thought this temple was empty."

"We need to find William." Oliver began to pace nervously. "I hope Charles didn't destroy him."

"But we thought Charles was destroyed," said Ezra.

"No," said Oliver, "he's the one who trapped me down here. This is his stronghold. We should probably try and make our way out of here. We don't want him finding us."

"Too late!" a voice called from the dark hallway.

"It's six against one! You don't have a chance. But we're not going to fight you anymore," Julian shouted. "We're going to tell the Overworld how you trapped a world-famous explorer and they will deal with you."

"They'll never find me." Charles splashed a potion of invisibility on himself and disappeared.

"Do you think he trapped William, too?" asked Oliver.

Harriet and her friends stood beside him, in awe. They couldn't believe they were actually meeting the famous explorer who had created most of the maps of the Overworld.

"The Overworld is going to be so excited when they find out you are alive," said Harriet. "People have been talking about your disappearance forever. There will be parades and many celebrations."

Oliver looked at Harriet. "I can't celebrate until we bring William home. I have to hope that he isn't destroyed and Charles has him trapped somewhere in the Overworld. And it's my mission to find him."

Julian and Ezra vowed to join Oliver in his quest to find William. "I don't know where he is, but I will help you," said Julian. "I will never forgive myself for selfishly choosing to travel to the End, and leaving both you and

William. I spent my life living with that regret and I will do anything to help find William."

"Thank you." Oliver smiled at his old friend.

Harriet and her friends also wanted to continue their search for William. "We've been searching for both of you all this time," said Harriet. "We would like to continue our search."

"And," Jack added, "we have a copy of William's first journal."

Toby said quickly, "It's what led us to you. But we finished it and we reached you, but it doesn't say anything about William."

"There are some pages missing," said Harriet.

Julian pulled the second journal from his inventory. From it, he pulled the missing pages. "I thought this book was a hoax, but I started to read it last night and I think I have to share these with you. I believe it can help us find William."

The group crowded around Julian as he read the loose pages.

18
JOURNAL ENTRY: A CALL FOR HELP

Trip 9: HELP!

I have waited for Julian and Ezra to return, but they haven't shown up. I've built a small house in the desert and every day I search for Oliver. I miss my friend and feel like the world of exploring is over for me. It seems empty and pointless without Oliver. I feel helpless because I can't find him. But I won't give up.

Today I spotted someone walking by the desert temple. At first I thought it was Oliver and hurried over, but on closer inspection, I realized it was Charles. I hadn't seen him in so long I had almost forgotten what he looked like.

"William!" Charles called out. "You're next!"

When he uttered these words, I knew he had destroyed Oliver. My heart sunk, but I was also filled with anger. I wanted revenge and I grabbed my diamond sword and lunged at him. But he crafted a portal to the Nether. A purple mist filled the sky.

I thought he had created it as a place to flee, so I was surprised when he shouted, "Pass through the portal!" to me.

"Never!" I shouted, coming at him again with my sword.

"If you ever want to see your friend Oliver again, you will come with me."

And there it was. If he was telling the truth, if there was any chance of saving Oliver, I had to face my fears and travel to the Nether.

Together we passed through the portal and emerged in the Nether. He led me to a Nether fortress. The trip the fortress wasn't easy, but I will spare you the gory details and the many attacks from fiery mobs. Luckily, I had a bunch of snowballs in my inventory. Once we reached the fortress, Charles trapped me. If anyone is reading this, I promise to reverse any curses associated with reading my journals. Please come and find me!

DO YOU LIKE FICTION FOR MINECRAFTERS?

Check out other unofficial Minecrafter adventures from Sky Pony Press!

Invasion of the Overworld

MARK CHEVERTON

Battle for the Nether

MARK CHEVERTON

Confronting the Dragon

MARK CHEVERTON

Trouble in Zombie-town

MARK CHEVERTON

The Quest for the Diamond Sword

WINTER MORGAN

The Mystery of the Griefer's Mark

WINTER MORGAN

The Endermen Invasion

WINTER MORGAN

Treasure Hunters in Trouble

WINTER MORGAN

Available wherever books are sold!

LIKE OUR BOOKS FOR MINECRAFTERS?

Then check out other novels by Sky Pony Press.

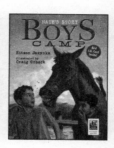

Pack of Dorks
BETH VRABEL

Boys Camp: Zack's Story
CAMERON DOKEY,
CRAIG ORBACK

Boys Camp: Nate's Story
KITSON JAZYNKA,
CRAIG ORBACK

Letters from an Alien Schoolboy
R. L. ASQUITH

Just a Drop of Water
KERRY O'MALLEY
CERRA

Future Flash
KITA HELMETAG
MURDOCK

Sky Run
ALEX SHEARER

Mr. Big
CAROL AND MATT
DEMBICKI

Available wherever books are sold!